Don't Spill the Beans!

Ian Schoenherr

Greenwillow Books · An Imprint of HarperCollins Publishers

With love to Eliza Gray Retter

For information address HarperCollins Children's Books,
a division of HarperCollins Publishers,
10 East 53rd Street, New York, NY 10022.
www.harpercollinschildrens.com

Permanent ink and acrylic paint on watercolor paper
were used to prepare the full-color art.
The text type is hand lettered.

Library of Congress Cataloging-in-Publication Data

Schoenherr, Ian.
Don't spill the beans! / by Ian Schoenherr.
p. cm.
"Greenwillow Books."
Summary: A bear tries hard to keep a birthday surprise a secret.
ISBN 978-0-06-172457-2 (trade bdg.) — ISBN 978-0-06-172458-9 (lib. bdg.)
[1. Stories in rhyme. 2. Birthdays—Fiction. 3. Secrets—Fiction. 4. Bears—Fiction.
5. Animals—Fiction.] I. Title. II. Title: Do not spill the beans!
PZ8.3.S3695Do 2010   [E]—dc22   2008042363

10 11 12 13 SCP First Edition 10 9 8 7 6 5 4 3 2 1

 Greenwillow Books

What's THAT, Bear?

A secret?

Don't spill the beans!
Don't let it slip!
Don't give it away!
Just button your lip!

Can't bear it?
Can't hold it tight?
Need to share it?

Oh...all right....

Tell
Elephant

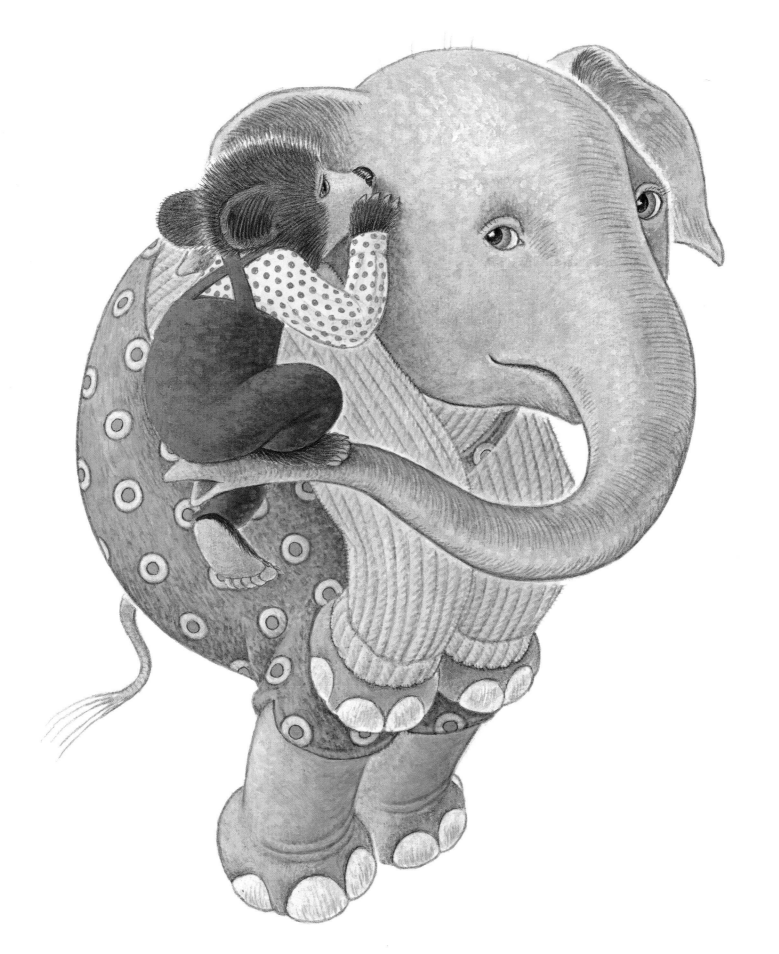

and Toucan, too.

Talk to Auk

and Kangaroo.

Blurt it
to Turtle.

Also Baboon.

Blab it
to Rabbit.

Alert Raccoon.

Tip off
Hippo.

Break it to Bat.

Leak it to Beaver,

to Lemur, to Cat!

Well, Bear, THAT was fun, but didn't you forget someone?

Please!
A peek!
A hint!
A clue!

Just spell it out!